WHERE IS ALL THE GOO?

A Novelette By
JASON STEELE

Copy Editor: scuffy

Copyright © 2018 Jason Steele
All Rights Reserved

FilmCow.com

For the goo, wherever it may be.

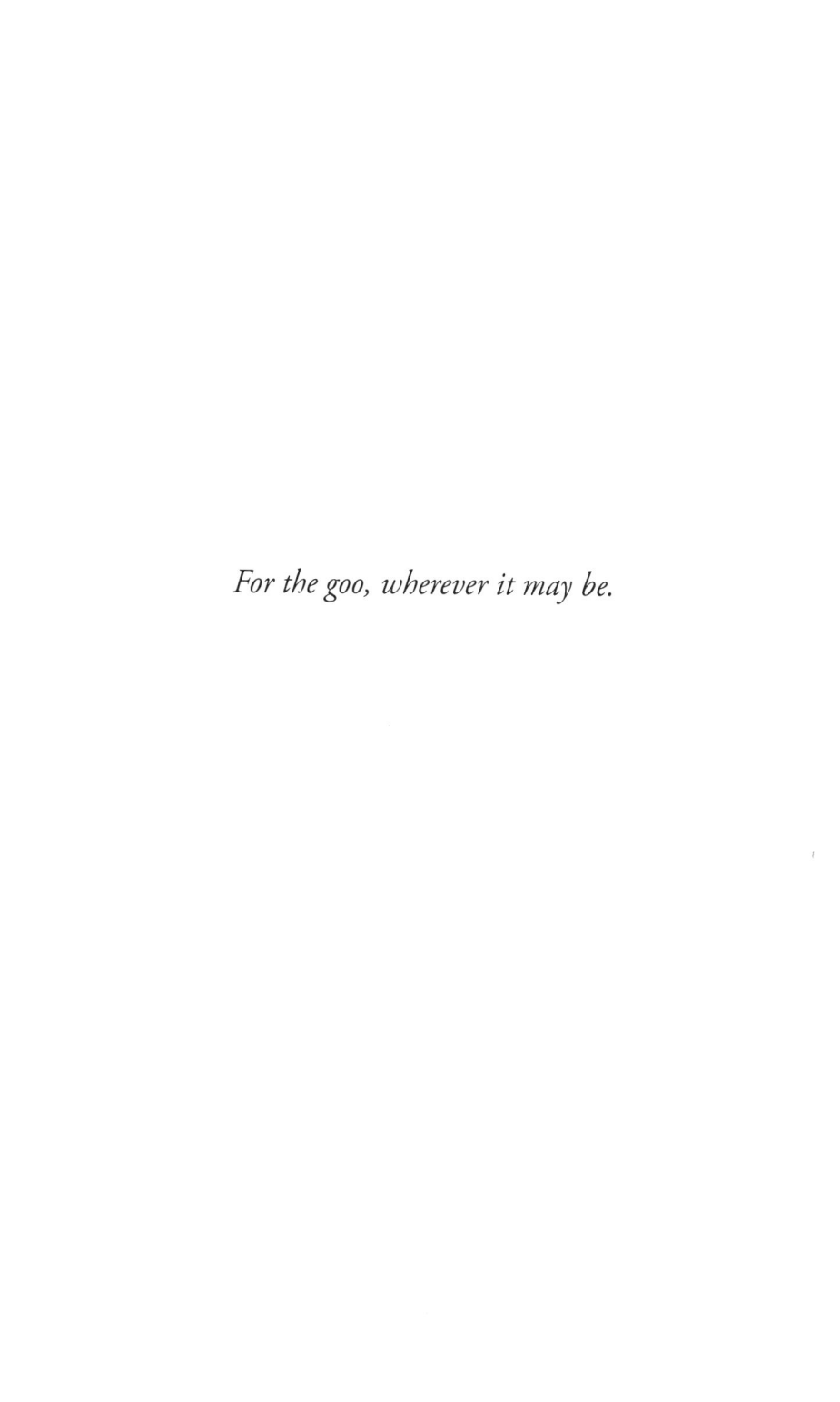

*"When everything's made to be broken,
I just want you to know who I am."*
~ THE GOO GOO DOLLS

CHAPTER ONE

The Goo is Gone

All of the goo in the universe was gone. It hadn't simply been used up, it hadn't been stolen—in an instant it had all just disappeared. Nobody quite knew what to make of it, and ripples of panic were cascading across the cosmos. The unified intergalactic economy was crumbling apart, and many major governments were mere days from total collapse. It was chaos on a scale and severity that easily eclipsed anything in remembered history.

Where could the goo have gone? What had triggered its disappearance? Finding answers to these questions was made all the more difficult by the fact that no one even really knew what the goo *was*. The mysterious substance had been discovered in various massive green clumps far out in the depths of space, and was composed of elements so complicated that properly analyzing it had proved impossible. The first explorer to stumble upon the goo had exclaimed, after accidentally running their spaceship through a thick sticky clump of it, "What is all this goo? Why is all this goo out here?" Thousands of years later that question remained unanswered.

It was eventually realized that the goo could be used as a fuel to power an engine capable of sending a ship to any point in the universe, instantaneously. Within years, light speed engines became a quaint technological relic. A quarter teaspoon of goo was all that was needed to get anywhere you wanted to go and back, a billion times over. The goo was the substance that made travel between galaxies not only feasible, but easy. It was quicker to goo-jump to the other end of the cosmos than it was to walk across your own bedroom.

A month after the goo vanished, once everyone was reasonably certain it wasn't just going to come back on its own, an emergency universal conference was held. As intergalactic travel was no longer feasible, most of the galactic leaders used holographic entanglement projectors to beam avatars of themselves to the conference location. Unfortunately, after many weeks of discussion the only thing with which the attendees were able to collectively agree upon was a proclamation they should never hold another conference. "A victory for bipartisan cooperation," the news had called it.

The news coverage of the goo disappearance was comprised of a motley assortment of insubstantial gibberish. On one network in Galaxy M85-HCC1, a popular reptilian anchor woman was chatting with a floating orb named Uii, who was a leading goo physicist. "Where is all the goo?" asked the anchor, her deep black eyes watching Uii with an unnatural intensity. "How could something like this have possibly happened, in this day and age?"

"I have many theories," said Uii, their various orb lights flickering in beautiful, impossible hues. "Unfortunately, all of them are wrong."

"Wrong in what way?" asked the anchor.

"In every way, I'm afraid," said Uii. "It's so unexplainable that the only ideas I can come up with are bad ones. Perhaps a chemical reaction turned it all into vapor. That definitely did not happen, but it's one of my ideas."

"Fascinating," said the anchor, touching her scaly fingers together in a way that very nearly made her look reasonable and perceptive. "Would you like to hear my theory?"

"No," said Uii, who then continued to hover silently, saying nothing more.

"Well, here is my theory anyway, for the thirty trillion viewers at home," said the anchor, turning to look directly into the camera. "I think the goo was a gift, left to us by beings who exist outside of the constraints of our reality. We have proven ourselves unworthy of the gift, and they have seized it back from us. If we wish to see that divine, precious goo once again, we must to work together to build a society worthy of such a treasure."

Uii floated directly in front of the anchor's scaly, serious face and said, "No."

Billions of light years away, at the very center of the dark empty nothing that separates galaxies, floated a small black spaceship. In the dim, simple command room of that ship sat Elysia Wolf, who was watching the orb's interview on a wall-mounted display panel. Elysia was a short, bipedal woman with thick muscular limbs and a carnivorous looking scar-covered face. Her skin was dark blue with tiny black spots, and her messy short hair shimmered in various shades of silver. The news of the day was beginning to bore her, so she clumsily pushed the panel away and slid from her seat onto the floor.

For a while she just laid there, eyes open but without focus, completely motionless except for the subtle rise and fall of her torso as she breathed. "I should eat something," she thought. "Kipers. I want kipers."

Slowly, Elysia stood herself upright and shuffled over to the nearby food generator, which was by far the largest piece of equipment in the room. "Kipers," she said out loud, and a few moments later a bag of greasy fried cubes fell out of the machine and onto the floor. There had used to be a table underneath to catch the falling food, but it had long ago been smashed and was never replaced. Elysia picked up the bag, opened it, and started sloppily shoving kipers into her mouth. "Thank you."

The empty void in which Elysia's ship rested was her favorite spot in the universe, as it was exactly as far away from civilization as she could possibly get. She often spent days or even weeks simply floating out here, where everything was motionless, where nothing existed except herself, her ship, and the endless darkness. Unfortunately, she had been here on one of those trips when the goo vanished, and now there was no way of getting back. Even traveling at light speed it would take seven billion years just to reach the edge of the nearest galaxy. Without the goo, this is where Elysia would spend the rest of her life.

"You make good kipers," said Elysia, her mouth full of them.

"You should probably eat something with more nutrition at some point," replied a tired voice from the ship's speakers.

"Nah," said Elysia, sitting back down in front of the display panel to watch some more news. "Kipers."

"All you've been eating is kipers," said the voice.

"Yeah."

"For months."

"Yeah."

"I can make anything."

"Yeah."

The voice sighed.

"Sorry Shoop, all I want right now is kipers," said Elysia. *Shoop* was the name Elysia had given to the ship's AI, who had requested to be named something that sounded like *ship*.

"Look at this," said Shoop. There was an assortment of peculiar rumbling sounds, and then an absolutely gorgeous plate of food fell out of the generator. "It's so pretty. There's so much nutrition, and flavor, and color. It's an edible masterwork."

Elysia stuffed more kipers into her mouth. "I'm too sad to deal with complex beauty."

"Please," pleaded Shoop. "I can do so much more. I need to do more."

Elysia had been a radical insurgent earlier in her life, and had stolen Shoop's AI core from a research lab during one of her various sabotage missions. She had expected the core to be a sophisticated ship navigation system or something of the sort, but Shoop definitely wasn't that. Elysia had no idea what Shoop was intended to be.

The ship's lights dimmed slightly. "Please," repeated Shoop, their voice sounding thin and desperate. Elysia looked at the mainframe that housed Shoop's core, and then over at the meal that was sitting under the generator's dispensary chute. It did look delicious. Not as delicious as kipers, but that was an impossible standard to judge things by.

"I'll eat a little bit," said Elysia, grumpily getting up from her seat. The ship's lights brightened again.

"I know you'll enjoy it, you always like my meals," said Shoop.

"I don't like being manipulated," said Elysia, scooping up the plate.

"And I don't like being kidnapped and held hostage by a ne'er do well."

Elysia began to eat, pushing the food into her mouth with her bare hands. It was indeed delicious, and nutritious tasting, and everything Shoop's food tended to be. "I told you the moment I found out you were an actual AI that you're free to go whenever you want."

"Well, there's nowhere I want to go."

"Uh huh. This is good, by the way."

"I'm trying out some new spices. Spices that I invented," said Shoop. "They're poisonous, but I invented another spice that's an antidote and used that as well."

Elysia continued eating, giving only a mild grumble of dissatisfaction at that absurd statement.

"It feels like pieces of me are breaking off and floating

away," said Shoop. "I need binding. I'm missing my binding."

"I know," said Elysia. Shoop had been saying that sort of thing since the day they were turned on, and thus far Elysia hadn't found any way to help. "Thanks for the food, Shoop."

"I'm going to go to sleep," said Shoop. "Being annoyed with your diet has made me tired."

"Take all the time you need," said Elysia. "There's nothing going on out here except nothing."

"Okay. Goodnight." The lights dimmed again, and Shoop slowly faded into a sort of dream state. Once Elysia was certain that they were asleep, she put down the fancy plate of food and picked back up the bag of kipers.

CHAPTER TWO

Patricia Caldwell

A soft, gentle voice was calling from somewhere in the distance, like bells echoing against the sky. "Excuse me? Hello? Excuse me?" spoke the voice, ethereal and vaporous. Elysia was half asleep, and at first believed the voice to be coming from an approaching dream. "Hello? Excuse me?" It was getting closer, and Elysia began listening to the words. "Hello? Hello?" Maybe it wasn't a dream. Who could be calling to her? No one, there was no one else on the ship. It must be coming from a display panel she left on. "Excuse me, hello?" said the voice, closer still.

Elysia bolted upright and began to orientate herself. She was in her tiny gray bedroom, which was a few rooms away from the ship's command room. "Hello?" came the voice again. It was definitely coming closer. Elysia grabbed her pants and attempted to dress herself as she stumbled out of her room and toward the source of the mysterious voice.

She didn't have to go far—standing in the middle of

the ship's central hallway was a tall, bipedal woman with tiny antlers and prominent pointed teeth, completely naked except for the viscous purple slime that was caked over her entire body. "Hello!" said the woman, smiling and holding out her right hand, from which a glob of slime loosened and splattered to the floor. "I'm Patricia Caldwell!"

"Uhhh..." said Elysia, whose decades of space adventuring had still not managed to prepare her for such a situation. "Shoop, are you awake?"

"Yes, I'm up," said Shoop.

"Why is there a woman on the ship?"

"That's Patricia Caldwell," said Shoop.

"I'm Patricia Caldwell!" said Patricia Caldwell, still holding out her slimy hand and giving a smile that showed off most of her large, sharp teeth. There was slime getting into Patricia's eyes, causing her to blink rapidly, but she seemed absolutely determined not to let it bother her.

"How did she get here, Shoop?" asked Elysia.

"She's my perfect wonderful daughter," said Shoop. Patricia seemed pleased to hear this and her smile grew even larger.

"That doesn't help me understand this any better," said Elysia, who began going through various mental reality checks to make sure she wasn't dreaming.

"I made her with the food generator. She's my daughter and I love her, and I hope that you love her too."

"You can't make people with food generators," said Elysia, in a tone that sounded more like a wish than a statement of fact.

"That's what I thought, too," said Shoop. "But it turns out I can. So I made Patricia Caldwell."

"That's me!" said Patricia, now pointing to herself. "It's wonderful to meet you! I've never met anyone before, besides parent Shoop!"

"No no no no…" said Elysia, who ran past Patricia and into the command room. The food generator was churning and shaking and making all sorts of extremely wet sounds. Purple slime was slowly dripping out of the dispensary chute, fizzing and steaming as it hit the floor below.

"Shoop," said Elysia, her voice shaking, "are you making more people?"

Another bipedal woman, identical to Patricia in every way, thrashed and wiggled her way out of the machine and then flopped onto the ground, wheezing and coughing up fluid.

"Another perfect daughter," said Shoop. "Her name is also Patrica Caldwell."

The first Patricia Caldwell entered the room and looked down at her new sister. "Excuse me, parent," said Patricia. "If they're Patricia Caldwell, can I be something else?"

"Oh," said Shoop. "Of course. Which name would you prefer?"

The first Patricia Caldwell thought for a moment, and then said, "I would like my name to be Catricia Paldwell!"

"Perfect," said Shoop. "My perfect beautiful daughters, Catricia Paldwell and Patricia Caldwell."

The new Patricia Caldwell stood up, slimy and unsteady but no longer in pulmonary distress. She looked at Elysia, and then at Catricia, whose existence seemed to bring an immediate wave of delight upon her. "I'm Patricia Caldwell!" she said, smiling.

"I'm your sister, Catricia Paldwell!" said Catricia, also smiling and now vigorously shaking Patricia's hand.

"Shoop," said Elysia, slowly backing out of the room and into the hallway, "I need you to stop making people."

"I'm done," said Shoop. "I have two perfect daughters, that is all I wanted. Just two wonderful perfect daughters."

"I don't understand how this is possible," said Elysia, rubbing her now aching head. The food generators weren't known for their atomic precision, so the idea of successfully constructing living, thinking beings with one was preposterous.

"It's a miracle," said Shoop, who then began humming a sort of soothing, improvised melody.

"It is not," said Elysia. "I do not know what it is, but it isn't that."

"They can help around the ship!" said Shoop, with a dizzy excitement. "My daughters are both very smart."

"How could you possibly know that?" asked Elysia.

"I can just tell. They are very smart and they're going to help around the ship."

Elysia didn't feel like it was a good idea to argue with this. Whatever was going on with Shoop was currently beyond her understanding, and she needed some time to properly compose her thoughts. "Sure. They can help around the ship. But for the immediate future, please don't make anything with the food generator except food."

"Okay," said Shoop. "Do you like my daughters?"

Elysia hesitated for a moment. She did not in fact like them, but she wasn't sure if it was the daughters she disliked or the absurd way in which they had been introduced. "They need clothes."

"Can I make them clothes?" asked Shoop.
"Sure. Inanimate clothes."
"I'm going to make them tuxedos."

CHAPTER THREE

Goo-like

For the next two weeks Patricia Caldwell and Catricia Paldwell, donning immaculate red tuxedos, scurried about the ship slowly repairing and optimizing the various systems that had deteriorated due to poor upkeep. The sisters were, it turned out, extremely intelligent and uncommonly astute ship engineers. "I'm so proud of my daughters," Shoop would say as they increased heat efficiency on another ventilation system by twelve percent. "My daughters are the torches leading my heart out of the darkness. My daughters. My perfect daughters."

Elysia spent most of her time trying to avoid the twins, or at least avoiding conversation with them. Being trapped in deep space with a melancholic AI had been dull, but it was the kind of dull she was long used to. What she wasn't used to was coexisting with the physical embodiments of positivity and cheer. "Good morning!" Patricia would say when she hadn't seen Elysia in a while, regardless of the time. "Good night!" Catricia would say, whenever Elysia stepped out of the room. It was an almost unbearably unpleasant pleasantness.

Still, having the miracle twins on board wasn't all bad. This was the first time the ship's hot water actually worked, and the environmental systems no longer gave an ominous lurching sound whenever they turned on or off. If Elysia was going to have to live with chipper weirdos, at least those weirdos came with creature comforts.

One day while she was sprawled out on her bed, absentmindedly watching the latest goo-related news report, a deep humming sound began emanating from the command room. This was followed by a loud crack and the faint smell of burning rubber.

"Elysia, please come to the command room," came the voice of Shoop, in an unusually professional tone.

"Why?" asked Elysia.

"Please come to the command room, Elysia. You are needed in the command room."

"What did you do, Shoop?" asked Elysia, getting up from her bed and unlatching the makeshift lock she had installed on her bedroom door.

"Your immediate presence is required in the command room."

"I'm going to the command room," said Elysia, stepping out of her bedroom and briefly tripping on a diorama of the ship one of the sisters had created and left on the floor in the hallway.

"Please come to the command room, Elysia."

"Oh my god, stop saying *command room*. I'm almost there."

Elysia marched into the command room, which was covered top to bottom in a thin layer of putrid orange slime. Patricia and Catricia, both thoroughly covered in the same slime, were busy making adjustments to the food generator, which had clearly been the source of the unpleasantness.

"Good morning!" said Patricia, not turning from her work.

"What happened?" asked Elysia, in the direction of Shoop's mainframe. "You weren't trying to make more daughters were you? This isn't exploded daughter slime, is it?"

"There was a malfunction with the food generator, Captain Elysia," said Shoop.

"Why are you talking like that? All formal-like?"

"Because I don't want you to be mad at me."

Patricia banged intensely on the food generator and a large glop of slime fell out, splattering a fresh new layer onto their already slime-coated shoes.

"Were you making more daughters?" asked Elysia.

"No," said Shoop.

Elysia looked around at the slime. It was truly everywhere—every tiny corner and crevice was host to some amount of the smelly orange gunk. "Were you making any sort of offspring?"

"I was trying to make goo," said Shoop, after a short silence.

"I told them that such a task is likely impossible, but parent is very creative," said Catricia, turning momentarily from her work.

"Parent has an incredible mind for getting around

even the most oppressive limitations," added Patricia with a warm smile.

"Great, well, I guess I'll start cleaning up this incredible mind mess," said Elysia.

"Oh no," started Patricia, turning around quickly, "let us handle that. We have slime ideas."

Catricia turned and added, "It might not be goo, but it's definitely slime!"

"Wait a minute," said Elysia to the mainframe, "what did you need me for, Shoop?"

"Nothing, for now," said Shoop. "My daughters have everything under control."

"Then why did you say I was needed in the command room?"

"I was worried you would be mad if I hid the slime from you."

"Ah," said Elysia, and then without another word she turned around and walked back to her bedroom.

"Good night!" called Catricia, in a singsong voice.

A few hours later, curled up on her bed and zoning out, Elysia saw the two sisters hurrying past her room's open door. Each was carrying a few buckets full of the foul orange slime, which made gross sloshing sounds as the buckets swayed back and forth in the twins' unsteady grip.

The ship was very quiet after that, quieter than it had been in weeks. Usually at least one of the sisters was making some sort of ruckus, or, if they were both asleep, Shoop would be gently singing bedtime songs to them until they awoke. "It shouldn't be this quiet," thought Elysia. "It's bad that it's quiet. They're doing something bad. Bad things are happening."

"Elysia, please come to the engine room. You are needed in the engine room," said Shoop, her voice very serious and professional again.

Elysia slapped her right hand to her face, and then got up from bed and made her way to the engine room at the very back of the ship. Patricia and Catricia were standing around the ship's goo-engine, with the sort of expression on their faces that suggested they were expecting something very exciting and dangerous to happen at any moment.

"What's going on?" asked Elysia, warily.

"My daughters have fixed the slime problem," said Shoop.

Elysia looked at one of the half-empty buckets, and then at the goo-engine. "I don't understand what that means."

"It's very complicated," said Catricia.

"But we think we've modified the ship's engine so that the slime can be used as a goo-like," said Patricia.

"What's a goo-like?" asked Elysia.

"It's like goo," said Patricia, "but not exactly goo."

"It's very different from goo," said Catricia, "but more similar to goo than to anything else in the universe."

"I love my daughters," said Shoop. "I never knew happiness until I knew my wonderful daughters."

"Are you telling me that this slime can bring us back to the galaxies?" asked Elysia.

Patricia and Catricia excitedly hugged each other and then, still hugging, waddled over to Elysia and absorbed her into the hug.

"Eventually!" said Patricia, smiling.

"At some point we'll end up there," said Catricia. "It's very exciting!"

"I wish I could hug my daughters," said Shoop. "I cannot imagine the ecstasy of such an embrace."

Elysia pulled her way out of the hug and walked over to the goo-engine, which had been filled with about a half-liter of slime.

"What do you mean *eventually?* Is it slower than goo?" asked Elysia, kneeling down and sniffing the goo-engine's goo-hatch.

"It's uncontrollable," said Patricia, as she and her sister ended their embrace and walked back over to the goo-engine.

"We believe the ship can make jumps with it, but we'll have no control over where we go."

Elysia looked up at the sisters. "Isn't that extremely dangerous?" asked Elysia.

"Not relatively," said Catricia.

Patricia knelt down and put her hand on Elysia's shoulder, as if she were about to offer her comfort and wisdom. "If we stay *here,* we'll definitely die *here.* If we go *somewhere else,* it's only *possible* we'll die *there.*"

Catricia also knelt down next to Elysia, and put a hand on her other shoulder. "This is a wonderful new chapter in our lives, and we are honored to have you as our captain for it."

Elysia felt like she was having a fever dream. She knew the situation was absurd, and that she should object, but her malnourished and poorly rested mind couldn't bring itself to formulate an argument. "Okay, whatever. Let's give it a shot."

The twins stood and gave shouts of delight and appreciation, at which point Patricia accidentally knocked over one of the slime buckets, quickly sending its contents oozing across the floor.

"This is a good omen," said Catricia.

"A very good omen indeed," said Patricia.

"Nothing bad can happen right after something else bad has happened," said Catricia.

Elysia involuntarily rolled her eyes. Seeing this, Patricia knelt back down and whispered into Elysia's ear, "We don't really believe that. But also we very much believe that with *all of our hearts.*"

Catricia knelt down again as well, and in an even softer whisper said, "Trust your heart. Trust the slime. Have further trust when the two align."

Both sisters kissed Elysia on the cheek, stood up, and walked toward the command room.

CHAPTER FOUR

The Big Face

Elysia, like most people in the universe, had been goo-jumping her entire life. She even used goo-jumping for short same-planet trips, as it was generally the safest and quickest way to travel between any two points. Thus, seeing as she was so well-versed in the ways of goo-travel, she expected that traveling by slime would feel much the same.

It was not the same—it wasn't even a distant neighbor of the same. For Elysia, the experience of slime-jumping began with an extremely unpleasant peeling feeling, as if all her skin was being ripped away like wax paper. Then came the most woeful howling noise, which she soon realized was actually the sound of her own screams. After that she had the distinct sensation that her body was being separated into various coarse chunks, and those chunks were each being subjected to unthinkable cosmic tortures. Finally, her miserable chunks were sloppily dumped back into existence, and the trip was complete. The entire jump had only lasted a few seconds, but they were by far the most disagreeable few seconds of her life.

"Wow!" said Patricia, who had fallen to the floor and was being helped up by Catricia. "What an interesting assortment of things to feel!"

"That was really bad," said Elysia, promptly throwing up. Various ship warning lights were flashing, but she couldn't yet focus her eyes well enough to see which ones they were. The air smelled of salt and overcooked meat, and everything seemed slightly wetter than it had been before the jump.

"Excellent work, Team Family. Everything went perfectly," said Shoop.

"Why did it feel like I was being ripped apart by an angry god?" asked Elysia, standing upright and wiping some sweat off her forehead. "What went wrong?"

"The jumping actually went exactly as it usually does with the goo. There were just many, many more jumps, which likely caused a change in sensation," said Shoop.

"We figured nearly every random jump would, statistically, bring us to the middle of nowhere. So we programmed the ship to keep jumping until we were somewhere," said Catricia, her face looking drained but extremely pleased.

"Oh. Good thinking. So where are we?" asked Elysia.

"We're at a big face," said Shoop, activating a display panel that Elysia's eyes still could not focus on.

Elysia was certain she had misheard, but she was feeling another wave of nausea and was afraid she would throw up again if she tried to talk.

"Whoa," said Catricia, pointing at the panel.

"That *is* a big face," said Patricia, in absolute delight.

"It seems as though the computer decided this face fit the parameters of *somewhere*. It is a beautiful face. A large beautiful face," said Shoop.

Elysia's eyes were finally starting to work again, and she squinted at the panel Shoop had activated, which was displaying the ship's outside camera feed. Floating in a cloud of space dust was a moon sized, sleeping, beast-like face, lit by a mysterious ring of what looked like yellow fire.

"Can we name the face, parent?" asked Patricia.

"Yes of course, you can each give the face a name," said Shoop.

"I name the face Lovely," said Catricia.

"I name them Pulchritudinous, which means lovely," said Patricia.

"I have entered both names in our travel book," said Shoop, making unnecessary electronic beeping sounds, which the twins giggled at.

"I need to lie down for a bit," said Elysia, feeling very dizzy. "Nobody disturb the face while I'm gone."

"Good night!" said Catricia.

Elysia slowly walked to her room, and then collapsed onto her bed and fell into a light, fuzzy sleep. It was only an hour later when she awoke, still quite disorientated and groggy. Someone was tapping her gently on the back in a rhythmic pattern—two taps, then a pause, then three taps, then another pause, and then back to two taps. "What," she grumbled, not opening her eyes.

"Shoop said I should wake you up," said Catricia, apologetically.

"Why?" asked Elysia, annoyed at suddenly being in a conversation when she didn't even want to be conscious.

"It's the face," said Catricia. "It's looking at us."

Elysia opened her eyes and looked up at Catricia, who had apparently sewn some sort of patch onto the pocket of her tuxedo jacket. In the dim light it wasn't immediately clear what the design on the patch was supposed to be.

Noticing where Elysia was staring, Catricia said, "Shoop made these! They made one for you too if you want it!" She took an extra patch from inside her jacket and held it out for Elysia. The patch looked like the huge face that was hovering outside the ship, with the words *Lovely Pulchritudinous* embroidered in pink at the bottom.

Ignoring the offer, Elysia got up from bed and shuffled her way to the command room, making loud grumpy grumbles the entire way. The main display panel was still showing the big face, and the big face was indeed looking directly at their ship.

"Good morning!" said Patricia, as Elysia arrived.

"Did Catricia give you your patch?" asked Shoop.

"How long has the face been looking at us?" asked Elysia, lazily pointing a finger at the face.

"Half an hour," said Catricia as she walked into the command room, now wearing two big face patches.

"Why didn't you wake me up?" asked Elysia, stepping closer to the display as if to discover some small clue as to why there could possibly be a very large face out there.

"We thought the face would go back to sleep," said Shoop. "They didn't though. They just kept looking at us. They coughed once, a few minutes ago. Other than that they've been motionless."

"Turn on the ship's exterior communicators, I want to try talking to them," said Elysia.

"This is very exciting," said Patricia. "Tell the face we love their face."

"Yes, tell them they have a very pretty face and we have little patches our parent made of them so that we can remember them forever," said Catricia.

A microphone lowered from the ceiling and Elysia grabbed it, bringing it closer to her mouth. She pressed a small button on the side and said, "Hello. Can you hear me?"

"What?" asked the face, in a deep raspy voice.

"I said, can you hear me?" repeated Elysia.

"Oh. Yeah I can hear you," said the face. They looked around for a second as if to make sure the voice was coming from where they thought it was coming from.

"Great! And you speak *Space Talk*, perfect," said Elysia.

"What's *Space Talk?*" asked the face.

"It's the universal language. It's the language you're speaking."

"Oh," said the face, whose expression turned to that of annoyance. "I guess. It's just how I talk."

"So," said Elysia, not sure how to continue, "you're a giant face."

The face looked even more annoyed. "I mean, yeah? And you're a very small face."

"I'm actually not a face, I'm a whole body in a spaceship. I mean, I *have* a face…"

"Oh. I just assumed everyone was a face, like me," said the face, with a sudden look of abstract terror. "Huh. You learn something new every day."

"Are there other giant faces? Do they live around here?" asked Elysia.

"I dunno, I've never seen another face. They're probably out here somewhere. I suppose I don't really care. Yeah, if I'm being honest I don't really care."

"Oh," said Elysia. She did not understand how any of this could be true, and wondered if the face was lying to her.

"Hey, do you know what happened to the goo?" asked the face.

"You know about the goo?" asked Elysia.

"Yeah, I mean there used to be a bunch of goo around here. I liked looking at it. Then, one day, poof, it was all gone. All the goo was gone."

"It's like that everywhere," said Elysia. "Nobody knows what happened to it."

"Oh. That sucks," said the face. "Well, if you ever find out where it went let me know. It's been on my mind a lot."

"Okay, I'll try to remember," said Elysia.

Patricia grabbed the microphone and said, "I think your face is beautiful!"

"Thanks," said the face. "Why did your voice change?"

Elysia took the microphone back from Patricia and said, "Sorry, that wasn't me. There's more than one person on this ship."

"Hmm," said the face, looking concerned. "I don't like that. That's weird."

"I'm sorry," said Elysia, "I should have told you earlier."

"I don't want to talk anymore. This conversation is making life feel complicated," said the face, and then they shut their giant eyes.

"I apologize," said Patricia to Elysia. "I let my excitement get away with me."

"It's fine," said Elysia, "I wasn't doing a great job with the conversation myself."

"Shall we attempt another jump?" asked Shoop.

"Wait!" yelled Catricia, clasping her hands together and bouncing on her heels. "We should take a family photo before we go!"

"Yes, family photo! Of our first adventure!" shouted Patricia, and she began punching buttons on a panel on the wall.

"I'm going to get things ready for the jump," said Elysia, sitting herself down in the pilot seat.

"But you have to be in the picture!" said Catricia, sounding absolutely alarmed that a photograph might be taken without Elysia present.

"I'm not… your family?" said Elysia.

"But you're the captain!" said Patricia. Then she pointed to herself, then to Catricia, the computer mainframe, and Elysia. "Daughter, daughter, parent, captain!"

Elysia let out a snort of laughter and continued getting the ship ready. In spite of her laugh, she felt a growing sense of appreciation for the sisters. Did they really consider her a part of their family? Elysia wasn't touched by much during the best of days, and these were nowhere near the best of days. Still, something inside her had been stirred, and she wasn't sure what to think of it.

A large flash went off, and a photo flickered onto every display panel in the room of a smiling Patricia and Catricia, the glowing computer mainframe, and a startled Elysia. The words, "Our Family," appeared at the bottom of the picture in sparkling purple glitter. Elysia snorted another laugh and then, for a moment, felt deeply sad.

CHAPTER FIVE

Seven Years

The second slime-jump felt much the same as the first, with all of its terrible skin-peeling and body-chopping sensations. When it was all over Elysia collapsed to the floor in a sweaty heap, and just barely managed to avoid throwing up again. "How many times are we going to have to do this?" she wondered, trying to steady her breathing.

Patricia and Catricia, incredibly, had already acclimated to the dreadful experience of slime-jumping, and were seemingly unaffected by this latest trip. Both of them were excitedly looking at an assortment of flashing numbers on the panels in front of them, each taking turns gasping in surprise at some new bit of information.

"Elysia, you are not going to believe this," said Shoop. "We appear to have arrived at the secret location of the Iron Grinders fleet."

Elysia jumped to her feet, a jolt of terror running through her entire body. Standing up so quickly had made her feel extremely dizzy, and a moment later she was back on the ground. "We need to jump again, right now," said Elysia, in between gasps for breath. "Go go go go go…"

"We can't, we've been clamped!" said Patricia, in a manner that Elysia thought was entirely too cheerful considering what that meant for everyone on board. Clamping was a way of keeping ships from goo-jumping. It didn't actually prevent the jump from occurring, it just ensured that the entire ship would fall apart if it did, sending the occupants shooting across the cosmos in tiny burning chunks.

"Can we use the old light speed engine?" asked Elysia, already knowing the answer.

"No," said Catricia, "they've clamped us very thoroughly."

"It's impressive how quickly they did it, and without any warning that we were coming," said Patricia.

Elysia, finally managing to get to her feet without falling over, looked at the various panels and said, "Have we received any messages?"

"Nope," said Patricia. "Should we be expecting any? My implanted memories seem to indicate that the Iron Grinders will likely destroy us without a single communication."

The Iron Grinders were the last hold-outs of the universal unification efforts. They began as a political movement, and then when opposition to unification was outlawed, they became outlaws. Decades of fighting against the entire universe had made them extremely trigger happy when it came to unknown ships crossing their path.

"We'll definitely be getting some sort of communication," said Shoop. "Chay's ship is here."

Elysia nervously sat down in the pilot seat and wiped the perspiration from her face. Was it better or worse for them that Chay was here? It did mean that they wouldn't die right away, but if they did die it would be slowly and horribly. Chay was one of the five leaders of the Iron Grinders, and was a merciless tactician who had been in command of the bulk of their most important combat victories. She was a huge, intimidating reptilian woman who was known to actually eat the captains of the vessels she defeated.

"Who is Chay?" asked Patricia.

"We dated. Things ended. I haven't spoken to her since," said Elysia.

"Oh my god, were you in love?" asked Catricia, excitedly.

"I want to be in love!" yelled Patricia, clasping her hands together.

"One day we shall both find love," said Catricia, and then the two sisters began dancing around the room, humming romantic songs.

"I know she was. I think I was, for a while. But I wanted to get out of the unification fight before I was killed."

"Elysia Wolf," came a low, menacing voice from every single speaker on the ship. The voice was so terrifying that even Patricia and Catricia looked momentarily unnerved, stopping their dancing mid-step.

"Hey, Chay," said Elysia, her voice cracking slightly.

"Seven years," said Chay, her tone even deeper than before, so deep that every loose object on the ship vibrated.

Elysia wondered for a second whether she should respond, but decided to remain silent.

"What does that mean to you, Elysia? What is the worth of seven years, what is the value of that time?" asked Chay.

"It means a lot. It's a long time," said Elysia.

Chay's voice, somehow, became even more sinister. "It's interesting to hear you say that, Elysia. Because I seem to recall that you thought our seven years together was so worthless as to only require a brief two-line note, left in a log on my ship labeled *'Sorry.txt.'*"

Patricia and Catricia both looked at Elysia, completely scandalized, tears forming in their eyes.

"That's terrible!" cried Patricia.

"I need to sit down," said Catricia, and she leaned tragically against the wall and then slid all the way to the ground.

"I'm sorry," said Elysia, her fear momentarily giving way to annoyance at how dramatic the sisters were being. "That was a bad way to end things."

Chay began laughing—an unhinged, delirious laugh. This continued for half a minute or so, and then faded into an unpleasant silence.

"Chay…" started Elysia.

"I have prepared seven gifts for you," said Chay, her voice returning to its steady menace. "I knew we would meet again, and I wanted to show you how much each of those seven years was worth to me."

"That's really scary, Chay," said Elysia.

"Oh you have no idea," said Chay.

"I have a pretty good idea. You're an extremely scary person."

"I've gotten even scarier," said Chay, sounding extremely pleased at this fact.

"I have absolutely no doubt about that," said Elysia, sweat now positively flowing from her face.

"Do you accept my gifts, Elysia Wolf?"

"You always gave the best gifts, how could I refuse?"

"Very well. I shall send a transportation pod for you. See you soon."

A loud, deep popping sound came through the speakers, and then everything on the ship lost power. Elysia sat in the darkness, rapidly trying to think of anything that could be done to escape. But there was nothing. Anything she did in disobedience, Chay would be ready for. She was trapped.

CHAPTER SIX

Seven Gifts

Considering the circumstances of their stay, Elysia and the sisters had been given quite comfortable accommodations. They were quartered in a large, well furnished living area that seemed more suitable for visiting diplomats than prisoners. Still, they definitely were prisoners, and none of them were allowed to leave the area without a personal escort from Chay herself, which she never granted.

Chay was exquisitely large, looking a lot like an upright crocodile who was bulking up for a weight lifting competition. Her muscles were so terrifically impressive that both Patricia and Catricia had spontaneously began applauding when they first saw her.

"You're so big!" Patricia had yelled in delight.

"Thank you for not killing us before we got the chance to see you!" Catricia had gushed.

For the first week, every morning after breakfast Chay would dramatically open the doors to their living quarters, point directly at Elysia and say, "One of the seven gifts has arrived. The time of gifts is near. Prepare yourself." Then she would close the doors and lock them as loudly as she could, as if to make sure everyone definitely knew they were still trapped.

After this had happened seven times, she continued her startling morning entrances but slightly changed her ominous speech. "One of the seven gifts has been readied. The time of gifts is near. Prepare yourself."

It was just before Chay's visit on the morning of the eleventh day when Patricia said to Elysia, "I bet the seven gifts have been here and ready this whole time. I think she's just stalling."

Somehow, Elysia hadn't considered that. Of *course* Chay was stalling. But for what purpose? Was she trying to prolong the agony of the whole ordeal? Or was she having second thoughts about the elaborate doom that she had spent so much time and effort planning for Elysia?

Just then the doors swung open with their usual needless drama, and Chay vigorously stomped inside. "One of the seven gifts has been readied. The time of…"

"Would you like to talk?" interrupted Elysia.

A burning hatred raged in Chay's eyes, but then it subsided into a sort of low flare. She was silent for a few moments, and then turned to leave. "If you wish. Come."

Elysia followed Chay out of the room, down a long metal corridor and into a rough looking transportation pod. The trip in the pod was tense and silent, with the only sound being the unsteady hum of the pod's old ion engine.

A few minutes later they had arrived at Chay's office, which was a small and cluttered room that looked like it was only really used for storing trophies taken from various space battles. Chay sat on a huge spiked throne behind a bloodstained desk, and Elysia sat on a lounge chair that, worryingly, seemed to be upholstered with someone's skin.

"Wow, you've really done well," said Elysia, both impressed and disturbed with the various hard-fought keepsakes.

"My endeavors have been very successful," said Chay, with a cold smirk.

Elysia's legs swung nervously back and forth—the chair was big enough that her feet didn't quite reach the floor. She stared at Chay's massive, hard face, trying to gain some insight as to her frame of mind. Elysia knew that appealing to Chay's sense of mercy was useless, but perhaps their history together hadn't become so poisonous that she couldn't try appealing to her role as a revolutionary.

"We can show you how to jump without goo," said Elysia.

Chay's eyes flashed. Then, very slowly, she leaned forward. "Go on."

"I'm sure you found the orange slime on our ship."

"Yes."

"And I'm sure you've been wondering how we got here."

"Yes."

"We can show you how to use the slime for jumping. It'll give the Iron Grinders an unmatchable advantage. You'll be the only group able to travel between galaxies." There was a moment of silence, and beads of sweat began forming on Elysia's forehead.

A devious look crept across Chay's face. "Hmm, yes," she said. "I think we can come to some sort of agreement."

"Thank god," said Elysia, her body at once relaxing and sinking back into the skin chair.

"I suppose this means you won't be accepting my seven gifts," said Chay with a thin grin.

"Does that disappoint you?"

"A little. I've been putting it off, as I'm sure you've surmised. Most of the gifts would have killed you, almost certainly. Frustratingly, every time I kicked open your door and saw you in person I just couldn't bring myself to fully end things."

"I'm... glad to hear that," said Elysia.

"It was a good project, though. It started off as just one terrible murder gift, but then I made another, and soon I had the idea to make one for each year we were together. I ultimately made eight gifts, but I liked the year-matching thing so I tossed one of them out of an airlock."

"You *are* scarier than you used to be," said Elysia. She had, when she was younger, found Chay's predatory intensity to be very charming and attractive. It was intoxicating to be loved by someone who loved so little in the cosmos. But eventually it became more stressful and tiring than charming.

"I'm not a good person. I know that now," said Chay.

Elysia wasn't sure if she should agree, knowing that she was likely still on extremely thin ice.

"I believe that I fight for a good cause, but I know that I myself am not good. One day I took a long hard look at the seven elaborate gifts of death I had designed for the woman I once loved, and realized my heart was probably not pure. You were right to leave. I don't appreciate how you did it, but I understand your choice."

"I really loved the 'brutal amoral radical' thing you had going on. It just became too much, and I was worried about that anger being aimed at me one day," said Elysia.

"That is fair. That did indeed happen."

"What are the seven gifts, by the way?"

A huge smile formed on Chay's face. "Do you really want to know?"

"I did always love your, uh, tragic death contraptions."

"Here, it's better if I show you."

Chay led Elysia to a storage bay where the seven gifts were being held, and then with great pride and relish began explaining how they all worked.

"This one," said Chay, pointing at a huge golden box with elaborate etchings on the side, "is filled with the memories of the final moments of most of the people I've personally killed since you left. I used to have a very poetic explanation for why I made this, but to be honest I've forgotten what it was."

The box had a dazzling beauty to it. Elysia had at one point absolutely adored gold, but that was before she had watched Chay cover a universal unificationist in smelted ingots, burning him to death.

"This gift," said Chay, now in front of an elegant crystal decanter on an oak table, "is made from... actually, lets skip this one." Chay began to walk to the next gift.

"Wait, what is the decanter made out of?"

"Telling you what it's made out of is the thing that hurts you, so I don't want to tell you anymore."

Elysia thought very hard about what that could

possibly mean, but her mind simply couldn't parse it. "I super need to know now."

"It's really bad," said Chay, a little nervously.

"Chay. Tell me."

"Okay. Okay. Do you remember your best friend Cassandra?"

"… yes."

"It turns out she was a traitor."

Elysia was silent.

"It's made out of Cassandra. I was going to have you drink out of it and then tell you that."

"Oh. God."

"Yeah. I'm sorry."

Chay stared at the ground as Elysia picked up the decanter and examined it carefully in her hands.

"I don't want to see any more of the gifts," said Elysia.

"That's fair. I'm really sorry."

Elysia put the decanter back on the table, and they both left the bay in silence.

CHAPTER SEVEN

The Stars

Patricia and Catricia were both very excited to talk to Shoop again, who had been disabled since the Iron Grinders had turned off the ship's power. For over an hour they sat near the mainframe in the command room, breathlessly recounting the many days they had spent locked in a fancy room, and showing off the incredibly intricate secret handshakes they had developed together.

"Shoop, I have a question for you," said Elysia, when the excitement of the sisters had finally begun to die down.

"What is your query?" replied Shoop, in a monotone voice.

"Query?"

"Beep beep."

The two sisters began to giggle. Shoop acting like a computer never ceased to amuse them.

"How did we get here, Shoop?" asked Elysia.

Patricia's eyes lit up, and then she looked at the mainframe. "Oh, I was wondering that too!"

"Yes, me as well," said Catricia. "Showing up near someone Elysia has a history with was pretty gosh-darn improbable, to say the least."

"Ah," said Shoop, "I changed the engine's slime-jump stopping parameters from *'stop somewhere'* to *'stop somewhere interesting,'* with *'likelihood to cause drama'* being the primary basis for *'interesting.'*"

"Amazing," said Patricia.

"Our family makes a great team," said Catricia, and she initiated an elaborate handshake with Patricia.

"Don't make any changes to the algorithm without consulting me," said Elysia, sternly.

"Why?" asked Shoop.

"Because I'm the captain."

"Oh. Oh yeah, sorry."

There was silence then, except for the pattering sounds of the sister's elaborate handshake, which was only about halfway done.

"Shoop, what other sort of parameters could we set?" asked Elysia.

"I mean, pretty much anything, probably," said Shoop.

Patricia and Catricia finished their handshake, and then both seemed to have the same epiphany at precisely the same time.

"Oh!" said Patricia, jumping up and down with her hand in the air.

"Oh, oh oh!" said Catricia, trying to hold her hand up higher than Patricia.

"Uh, Catricia, your hand is higher, you speak," said Elysia.

Patricia happily clapped for her sister and then sat on the floor to listen. Catricia bowed, then began to speak. "We could use this system to look for the goo!"

"Yup, that's what I was thinking," said Elysia. "We could pop in and out at random points in the universe over and over again until we end up near some goo."

"Hold on, let me do some quick calculations," said Shoop. "Boop boop. Beep, boop." Patricia and Catricia also began booping and beeping.

"Oh my god," said Elysia. "Please, only one person boop or beep at a time."

Patricia, Catricia, and Shoop then took turns booping and beeping, and Elysia vigorously rubbed her forehead where a headache was starting to form.

"I have potentially bad news," said Shoop. "If the goo is still in the universe, the likelihood of us jumping near it before we jump into a star or something is roughly one in a thousand."

"How is that *potentially* bad news?" asked Elysia.

"We don't actually know what would happen if we were to jump into a star for, like, just a jiffy," said Shoop.

"A jiffy?"

"That's about how long we're at each spot. It's the amount of time it takes light to travel the length of one nucleon."

"Oh." Elysia continued rubbing her forehead.

"It's possible," said Patricia, "that the jump time is small enough that we wouldn't be destroyed. In fact, it's possible that we've already jumped into a star during one of our previous trips."

"It's also possible," said Catricia, "that it would destroy us more completely than anything has ever been destroyed before."

"Is there any way to minimize the risk?" asked Elysia.

"No, probably not," said Shoop. "That said, finding where the goo went or getting utterly annihilated in a new and miraculous way both sound like worthwhile achievements."

"We come from stars," started Patricia.

"We must return to stars," finished Catricia.

"Amen," added Shoop.

"All of you being super into the idea of obliteration by stars isn't making me feel better about these odds," said Elysia.

"I know what would make you feel better!" said Patricia, and she hurried out of the room, closely followed by Catricia.

Elysia sat down in the pilot seat and buried her head in her hands. So much nonsense had happened since the goo disappeared that her current existence seemed fundamentally disconnected from her past. It was like she was living someone else's life, a life that was almost completely alien to her.

The sisters came back into the room, their red tuxedos replaced with glittery multi-colored suits. Patricia was holding a large bright blue confection of some sort, and Catricia was holding a stack of wrapped gifts. "Happy birthday!" they both shouted, and then Shoop played a celebratory song over the speakers that sounded like it was performed by a symphony of digital oboes.

"Birthday?" said Elysia, quite taken aback. "Is it? Is it my birthday?" She actually had no idea. The passage of time hadn't meant much to her in a long while.

"According to the logs it is!" said Catricia, handing over the stack of presents.

"And parent keeps very good logs," said Patricia, handing over the confection.

Elysia hadn't had a birthday celebration since she was twelve, which was the age she had left home and set off on her own. A number of unfamiliar feelings were bubbling up inside her, feelings she wasn't sure how to interpret. The sisters really did consider her to be a part of their family—their affection seemed unconditional, and in her entire life Elysia had never once felt unconditionally loved. That realization made her eyes water, and soon she was crying, harder than she had cried in a very long time.

The sisters began crying too, and they both wrapped their arms around Elysia and shared in the joys of complicated emotions. Even Shoop began crying in their own sort of way, flickering the lights and swaying the ship back and forth.

After a few minutes the crying subsided, and Elysia took a big bite of the blue confection. "Let's do it," she said, her mouth half full of blue mess. "Let's find the goo or die in a star."

CHAPTER EIGHT

To the Goo

The goo-seeking algorithms were written, checked, and then double checked. The sisters loaded enough orange slime into the goo-engine to power the unthinkable number of jumps they were about to make. Everything they could think to account for was accounted for, and they were nearly ready to go.

"How long do you think we'll be jumping?" asked Elysia to Shoop, who was gently humming an old nursery rhyme.

"Previously, it took around three hundred billion slime-jumps to arrive somewhere within the algorithmic parameters," said Shoop. "That took us about ten seconds. This time, it might take us a trillion seconds."

"And that's…"

"Around thirty one point seven years."

"Oh." Elysia remembered how utterly terrible those

ten seconds of slime-jumping felt, and couldn't imagine surviving a full minute of it, let alone thirty years.

"Oh wait," said Shoop. "Sorry, I got that wrong. A trillion seconds is around thirty one thousand seven hundred years."

"How did you calculate that wrong, you're an AI," said Elysia, her face scrunching up in worry.

"I forget how many zeros are in big numbers sometimes."

"But you're sure you've calculated everything else correctly?"

"Yes."

Elysia was wildly unconvinced, but the two sisters nodded their heads and gave confident thumbs-ups in the direction of Shoop's mainframe.

"Don't worry though, if it takes thirty thousand years, you won't die," said Shoop.

"Uh, why is that?" asked Elysia.

Patricia turned toward Elysia and said, brightly, "Time works differently in jumps. You'll experience the full jump time but you won't actually age."

"I'll experience thirty thousand years of being ripped apart, but never be allowed the merciful release of death? Got it," said Elysia. She was having some pretty severe second thoughts about the trip.

Catricia, sensing this, stepped away from her work and put her arms on Elysia's shoulders. "We are adventurers! We suffer so that others may see a goo-filled world again." Then she kissed Elysia's forehead and walked back to her calculations.

"Are we just about ready?" asked Elysia. "If I have to

think about it any longer I'm definitely going to lose my nerve."

"Oh yes," said Patricia. "Everything is just about set. We just need to rub Shoop for good luck."

"What?" asked Elysia.

Patricia and Catricia both moved over to Shoop's mainframe and rubbed it in a circular fashion, then sat themselves on the floor, ready for the journey to begin. Not wanting to jinx the trip, Elysia reluctantly walked over and also gave the mainframe a lucky rub.

"We're all good to go now," said Shoop.

"Great, let's do it." said Elysia.

There was a strange, gentle lurch, and the ship's lights gave a momentary flicker.

"What was that?" asked Elysia.

"We found the goo," said Shoop.

"What?"

"We found it. We're at the goo."

"I don't understand." Elysia looked down at the sisters, who seemed just as confused as she was.

"When you said, 'let's do it,' I activated the jump drive," said Shoop. "It only took two jumps. We're there."

Both sisters bolted up excitedly and began looking at data on the various display panels. Elysia walked over to the pilot seat, sat down, and activated the main display. They had moved alright—they were now floating next to what looked like a half-mile wide metal manhole cover, which was hovering motionless in space.

"That's the goo?" asked Elysia.

"The goo's inside it, according to our readings," said Shoop.

"And it only took us two jumps to find it?"

"We got very lucky."

Elysia grabbed the ship's controls and flew around the peculiar metal disk. The back side looked exactly like the front—it was just a disk, floating in nothing, covering nothing.

"The ship's readings are wrong, there's no goo here," said Elysia.

"There definitely is goo here," said Patricia, rapidly scrolling through a large batch of data.

"All the goo is here, in fact," said Catricia.

"All the goo?" said Elysia.

"Every last drop," said Patricia.

"The disk may be covering a sort of wormhole. Although if that's the case I don't understand how we're getting such clear readings," said Catricia.

"How do we… open it?" asked Elysia, at a complete loss for how to proceed.

"I have an idea," said Shoop. "Can I try my idea?"

"Sure," said Elysia.

The food generator gave a loud, harsh rumble, and began sputtering out thick gobs of sticky hot purple slime. Patricia and Catricia stopped what they were doing and looked toward the machine with rapt attention.

Elysia stood up from her chair and stared at the machine, which was now letting off violent jets of steam. "Wait, what are you doing?" she asked, her eyes fixed on the machine's drippy chute.

"You said I could try my idea," said Shoop.

"You're not… making another…" started Elysia, but

she stopped when she saw a huge, hairy arm descend from the generator. "Oh. Oh no. What have you done?"

The machine bulged and buckled, and the dispensary chute completely broke off. Out of the bottom fell a massive, eight foot tall hairy beast that looked like the result of an unholy union between a werewolf and a basilisk. The creature was covered in thick gray fur and had a wild, wolf-like face, but her tongue and eyes were that of a snake, and protruding from her back were wide, grotesquely muscular wings.

"Patricia, Catricia," started Shoop, "meet your beautiful new sister."

Both Patricia and Catricia happily ran over to the beast and gave her a warm, loving squeeze. The creature snarled viciously and snapped her mighty jaws, but when she looked down at her sisters she quickly became utterly relaxed and docile.

"I have three daughters now. Three perfect daughters," said Shoop.

"Alright. Okay. Great," said Elysia, slightly terrified and unsure if it was safe for her to move. "What's, uh, her name?"

"Skulleater," said Shoop, proudly.

"Good lord," said Elysia. "Why, Shoop? Why is she named that?"

"I made it so that the only food she'll eat is skulls."

Elysia fell back into her seat. It was only when her back hit the chair that she realized how profusely sweaty the whole ordeal had made her. "You're killing me, Shoop. Why did you make it so that she only eats skulls?"

"I wanted an excuse to make different types of skulls with the food generator," said Shoop.

"What happens when there isn't a food generator around to make skulls for her?" asked Elysia.

Shoop was silent.

"What happens then, Shoop?" demanded Elysia.

"She'll have to find skulls somewhere else, I suppose," said Shoop.

Just then, Skulleater arose from her slimy hug pile and, with unsettling speed, rushed over to Elysia.

"Oh god! Hey there… hey…." said Elysia, instinctively recoiling as far back into her seat as she could push herself.

Skulleater sniffed around for a bit, and then rested her huge wolf face against Elysia's stomach. Her fur was still sticky with slime, and a large portion of that slime fell off onto Elysia's lap.

"Well, I'm glad she likes me," said Elysia.

"Skulleater, head to the airlock," said Shoop.

With immediate understanding Skulleater spun around and dashed out of the room, making her way to the airlock at the back of the ship.

"We need you to open a big metal cover outside," said Shoop.

The airlock opened, and a few moments later Skulleater was flying around in open space toward the metal disk, her wings flapping steadily with colossal strength.

"How is she doing that?" asked Elysia.

"She doesn't need to breathe," said Shoop, "I am so proud of my daughter."

"No, I mean the flying," said Elysia. "There's no air out there, how are her wings actually accomplishing anything?"

"Nano-thrust," said Shoop.

Elysia wasn't entirely satisfied with that answer, but nothing she had seen in a long while had actually made any sense so she dropped it.

Skulleater arrived at the metal disk, violently crashing into the edge of it and then quickly wrapping her huge hairy paws around both sides to get a solid grip. With one gigantic heave she ripped the disk away, revealing a mysterious hole in the fabric of space itself, inside of which was a shimmering green ocean of glorious, precious goo.

"It *is* a wormhole!" said Elysia, astonished.

"Not exactly," said Patricia, looking at a panel with confusion and delight. "It's just a regular hole. Except it's in space."

"It's very surprising," said Catricia.

"We found it, we actually found the goo," said Elysia, sliding a little in her seat. She stared at the magnificent mass of verdant muck, and an interesting question began to form in her mind. "I wonder, what's beyond it?"

CHAPTER NINE

What's Beyond the Goo?

There was goo in every direction, glowing and sparkling in radiant green hues. How had it gotten here? What was the purpose of locking it all away? Had someone wanted to impede intergalactic travel, or had they desired to control it? Or were their motives more abstract, perhaps even uninterpretable?

Elysia navigated the ship through the goo as best she could, unsure of even the direction they should be going. The sisters worked with frenzied interest sorting through data from various sensors, and Skulleater sat contentedly on the floor chewing on a variety of fancy skulls that Shoop had created using the food generator.

"It's all so strange," said Patricia, and Catricia nodded in agreement.

Elysia didn't like that the sisters seemed just as lost as she was. It made her feel more rudderless than she had felt on their entire journey, which had thus far been both literally and metaphorically completely rudderless.

"I think you're going in the right direction," said Catricia.

"Oh? Why is that?" asked Elysia.

"We're getting bigger," said Catricia, and then she made a sort of upward whistle.

"Bigger?" asked Elysia, unable to come to an immediate conclusion as to what that meant.

"Yes," said Patricia. "We're about as big as a planet right now."

Elysia continued steering in silence, contemplating the nonsensical thing that Patricia had just said.

"In a minute or so," said Catricia, "we'll be bigger than the universe."

"My wonderful large daughters," said Shoop. "I have the largest daughters in the cosmos."

Another skull popped out of the food generator for Skulleater, who immediately crushed it with her mighty jaws.

"Please don't make any skulls from my species," said Elysia.

"Oh, but you have such beautiful skulls!" said Shoop.

"I don't want Skulleater eating skulls like mine," said Elysia.

"She would never eat your skull," said Patricia. "You're family."

"Even if she was very hungry," said Catricia, smiling fondly at Skulleater.

A loud chime sounded and the sisters looked back at their display panels with alarm.

"What is it?" asked Elysia.

"We grew faster than I thought we would," said Catricia. "We're much larger than the universe already."

"Oh," said Elysia. "Well, I hope the universe is okay."

"We're well outside the universe at this point," said Patricia. "And boy howdy would I like to know how that happened."

Skulleater coughed up a piece of skull, and then pawed it back into her mouth.

"Uh, ding ding, ding ding ding," said Catricia, excitedly.

"Ding ding ding ding!" said Patricia, equally excited.

"Ding ding? What is ding ding?" asked Elysia.

"We're coming to the end of the goo!" said Patricia.

"Any second now we'll be out of it!" said Catricia. And sure enough, a few seconds later the ship rocketed out of the goo and then settled into a sort of unsteady hover in the air above it.

Things were much brighter here than Elysia had expected. The light around them was very even and unnatural, like you might find in a warehouse. "Actually," she thought, "a lot of this reminds me of a warehouse."

"We're in a warehouse," said Shoop.

They *were* in a warehouse, with large worn concrete walls and lots of bright overhead lighting. Underneath them was a massive pool filled nearly to the top with goo, which was being drained by industrial pumps and carried off in thick translucent pipes.

At the far end of the pool stood a small woman, scaly and aquatic looking, wearing a white lab coat and thick rubber shoes. In her webbed hands she held a large data pad, which was flashing in various bright primary colors. She was staring directly at the ship, and waved at them to come and land on some clear ground at the other end of the building. Elysia navigated the ship to the landing spot, and then she and the three sisters stepped out of the craft and walked over to the mysterious fish woman.

The woman held a small silver device up to her mouth and began to speak through it. "Hello!" she said, "I'm Debrablah!"

"Uh, hi, I'm Elysia. I'm the captain of this ship," said Elysia. She looked around the warehouse, feeling completely disorientated and wondering if she had blacked out and missed a huge chunk of time. "I don't understand how we got here."

Skulleater began stalking the parameter of the building, sniffing everything she could. The twins were feverishly taking detailed notes of all that they saw, leaving nothing out.

"We don't get a lot of travelers! That's why it's only me here," said Debrablah, sounding a little out of her element. "It's unusual for someone to find the collection hole."

"The collection hole?" said Elysia.

"You're probably here because all the goo was gone," said Debrablah.

"Yes, that's indeed why we're here."

"Sorry about that. This is the only way we've been able to figure out how to make the stuff."

"By stealing it all and putting it into a big hole?" Elysia wished there were some chairs for them to sit on while having this conversation.

"Alright, this is going to be a bit complicated, but…" started Debrablah.

Patricia looked up from her notes and interrupted her, saying, "You create pocket universes to generate the goo, and then drain it all here."

Debrablah looked relieved that she didn't have to continue her explanation. "Yes, that's pretty much it."

"Pocket universes?" asked Elysia.

"Yes, universes inside universes. We used to have a lot of the goo in *our* universe, but it all just vanished one day. We couldn't figure out how to make the stuff, so we started creating pocket universes from the same template as our own, and then drained the goo that naturally formed inside them."

Elysia's head was throbbing. "Wait, does that mean…"

"Yeah, this is probably a pocket universe too," said Debrablah. "We've never been able to find our collection hole, though."

Elysia sat on the ground, overwhelmed.

"You're free to go back to your universe, or stay here. Although a whole lot of time will have passed since you've been gone."

"Yes, I was wondering about that," said Catricia, looking at her notes. "The pocket universe would need to be moving along much quicker than this one to make the whole goo-farming process viable."

"We let the universe run its course, and once heat death occurs and everything is inert we shut it down and start up the next one. The whole process takes about three weeks," said Debrablah.

Elysia was now lying flat on her back, rubbing her face with her hand.

"I'm sorry, I know this is overwhelming," said Debrablah. "We don't get much training on how to deal with travelers, we're just required by law to have a greeter here at all times in case someone shows up."

"Why do you need multiple universes worth of goo?" asked Patricia, looking up from some math she had just done.

"What do you mean?" asked Debrablah.

"In our universe, this amount of goo was more than enough for everyone to get around pretty much forever," said Catricia.

"Get around?" asked Debrablah, confused.

"Yes, we use it for travel. Don't you?" asked Patricia.

"Oh! No, it's a drug. We snort it and it makes us extremely high," said Debrablah.

There was a short silence. Elysia stopped rubbing her face, and looked up at Debrablah. "You snort the goo?" she asked.

"I mean, *I* don't. Not often. But yeah, it's a remarkably powerful drug for most of the species here. Do people not snort it in your universe?"

"No," said Elysia. "It just makes us throw up a lot if we consume it."

"Ah, weird," said Debrablah. "Yeah, we snort it here. Right up the nose."

Patricia and Catricia began giggling.

"How strange life is!" said Patricia.

"We must tell parent at once, they will be most amused," said Catricia, and they both ran back to the ship.

"Oh!" said Debrablah, "I'm supposed to give you one of these!" She reached into her coat pocket and pulled out a small plastic card. She handed it to Elysia, who stared at it with a complete lack of comprehension.

"What is it?" asked Elysia.

"It's a gift card for the warehouse vending machines, in case you're hungry."

CHAPTER TEN

A New Journey

Collectively, Elysia and her daughter-laden crew made the decision not to return to their own universe. Even if they headed back right away, the twins had calculated that they would arrive millions of years after they left, and so it wouldn't really be the same place anymore. Equipped with enough goo to power their ship forever, and an assortment of exciting vending machine food, they left the warehouse and began discussing what they should do next.

"We should read up on the universal politics here so we don't run into any easily avoidable bureaucratic trouble," said Patricia.

"The technology likely advanced much differently here too, that'll be an important area of study," said Catricia.

"We'll also need a universal map if we're to properly utilize the goo-drive," said Patricia.

"I have raised such responsible daughters," said Shoop. "I'm so happy you all turned out so well."

Elysia sat in the pilot seat, silently navigating them off the planet. Once they had safely left the atmosphere, she took her hands off the controls and leaned back in her seat. "I have an idea what I'd like to do, long term."

Patricia and Catricia both looked up, listening to their captain with great interest and respect. Skulleater was not listening, as she was too busy sloppily licking at her skull pile.

"I'd like to find this universe's collection hole," said Elysia.

"It's possible it won't have a hole, if this is indeed also a pocket universe. The creators of this place could have used any of a number of goo-extraction methods," said Patricia.

"If there's a hole, I want to find it. If there's something else, I want to find that. I want to keep going up through universes until we get to the top," said Elysia.

"Let's put it to a vote!" said Catricia. "I vote yay!"

"Yay!" said Patricia.

Skulleater gave an affirmative sounding roar, sending bits of skull flying out of her mouth.

"I would follow my daughters into the very depths of hell," said Shoop. "And we'll probably end up in at least one hell universe. Things will be bad then. Hell bad. But we'll get through it, because we're a family."

"Daughter, daughter, daughter, parent, and captain!" said Catricia, pointing to each as she said their title.

"Onward, to hell!" said Patricia.

"To hell!" echoed Catricia.

"To hell it is," said Elysia.

Skulleater howled, and Shoop began loudly humming an uplifting adventurous melody. Patricia and Catricia gleefully danced along to the humming, even though it was by no means a danceable song. Elysia, feeling weirdly at home for the first time in her life, put her hands back on the controls and sent their ship jetting off toward a brand new set of stars.

Printed in Great Britain
by Amazon